Benjamin Reynolds Bulkeley

The Shifting Wind & other Poems

Benjamin Reynolds Bulkeley

The Shifting Wind & other Poems

ISBN/EAN: 9783744722186

Printed in Europe, USA, Canada, Australia, Japan

Cover: Foto ©Andreas Hilbeck / pixelio.de

More available books at **www.hansebooks.com**

THE SHIFTING WIND

The Shifting Wind

&

Other Poems

by

Benjamin Reynolds Bulkeley

CHICAGO: MDCCCXCV

A NUMBER OF THESE POEMS HAVE BEEN PUBLISHED BEFORE IN VARIOUS PERIOD- ICALS. THE AUTHOR WOULD MAKE ESPECIAL ACKNOWLEDGEMENT TO MESSRS. HARPER AND BROTHERS FOR PERMISSION TO REPRINT THE SONNET "LOVE THE CROWN OF CREATION," WHICH APPEARED IN HARPER'S MONTHLY FOR NOVEMBER, 1889.

ERRATA.

FOR "ONE" READ "SONG" IN LINE 2 PAGE 16.

FOR "AUGHT" READ "OUGHT" IN LINE 7 PAGE 36.

THE SHIFTING WIND

Hark! now the fickle wind has turned
  And calleth loudly to my fire;
And through the gloomy chimney-place
  Summons the tongues of flame the higher.

And now responsive shadows play
  And dance about the lonely room
Until it seems that joy alone
  Could habit here instead of gloom.

Oh! yes, the winds have turned about
  And now are chasing from the west;
But oh! that Fortune's storm could change
  The tides within this troubled breast.

Cambridge, April 14, 1882.

SOWING AND REAPING

"One soweth, and another reapeth."—John 4:37.

Surely one man soweth
While another reaps;
And the mother waketh
While the baby sleeps.

Each one finds a harvest
Which he never sowed ;
Each one bearing burdens
Lifts another's load.

Every one is reaper
From some distant seed ;
Every one is sower
For another's need.

This is law and gospel !
Sweet it is to find
When the sowers perish
Reapers come behind.

Sowing and Reaping

Praise the God of Harvest:
  What is wrought in tears
Bringeth some one blessings
  In the mystic years.

Praise the God of Harvest
  That another reaps;
So the labor fails not
  When the sower sleeps.

Concord, Mass., November 19, 1882.

WE TWO

We sat beside the moonlit lake,
   My cherished friend and I.;
No sound our converse sweet did break,
   No other soul was nigh.

The burning day had given place
   To evening cool and fair,
And all things seemed our hearts to bless
   The while we lingered there.

We turned from burdens of the day —
   I know not hers, but mine
Were those but seldom stayed away,
   A weary daily line.

We turned from burdens of the day
   And dwelt that while apart
From stiff society to say
   The promptings of the heart.

We Two

So there the truest friendship threw
    Far off the formal cloak ;
Nor was there empty thought we knew
    Nor empty word we spoke.

We looked into each other's hearts
    And spake our meanings whole,
And, when some deeper theme would start,
    We talked from soul to soul.

It was not love, 'twas friendship pure
    That bound our feelings then —
A friendship which will rest secure
    Should we ne'er meet again.

Such friendship ne'er will find alloy
    In fortune's loss or gain —
If one but tread the hills of joy,
    The other vales of pain.

I know not if again may we
    That lakeward walk retrace,
Or if in life we e'er may see
    Again each other's face,

We Two

For now our ways are sundered far,
    Nor know I where may fall
The radiance of my fortune's star,
    Or if it shine at all.

I only hope there may return
    Some time such blessed spell;
And toward such hour I fondly yearn
    With wish I scarce may tell.

We sat beside the moonlit lake,
    My cherished friend and I—
No lot so hard can hap to break
    That memory till I die!

Cambridge, October 9, 1879.

BLOSSOMS

By my window there stands a tender tree:
　　Last night it blossomed so fair;
And to my couch its perfume, free,
　　Was brought by the evening air.

So it came in the hush of yesternight,
　　The first faint sense of my love;
And I said: "Can it be that the longed-for light
　　Has dropped from the urns above?"

From sleep I turned to the starry sky
　　And craved to know if a ray,
Newborn, had kindled another's eye
　　As restless as mine for the day.

And I said: "I will leave this anxious thought,
　　So sudden and strange it seems;
I'll wait and see if my lady be caught
　　In the tell-tale thread of my dreams."

Blossoms

And now the blossoms that burst in the night
    Lie fragrant and faint on the ground ;
And I shut them in memory's casket tight,
    But the fruitage will never be found.

Cambridge, April 27, 1882.

SONG

I hate to have the summer come
    Because it brings not thee;
The flowers that spring about my home
    Will whisper woes for me.

The rose will mock thy beauty's blush,
    The birds thy heavenly cheer;
And Nature's song, or Nature's hush
    Will say thou art not here.

Oh! would the winter might abide
    With naught to liken thee;
So I within its tomb might hide,
    Warmed by thy memory.

Cambridge, May 4, 1882.

GOD IN THE CALLING

O, the work I have chosen delights my soul
    Beyond all other employ;
And I linger in thought on its far-shining
     goal,
    And nothing my peace can destroy.

But if God should choose Him to take away
    The streugth which my life hath blessed,
Should I ply my new calling gladly each day
    As surely for me the best?

Chicago, April 8, 1895.

THE SADDEST OF THOUGHTS

The saddest thought that ever found its way
Into the curious chambers of the mind
Is, that to close the latest earthly day
Sums all of life; that all is final, blind
Dispose of elements, nor shall we find
Rest other than the dusty remnants have
Which were our bodies and the soul en-
    shrined,
Then to be parted like the unmeaning wave—
Unfriendly atoms all, forth wandering from
    the grave.

Chicago, November 30, 1878.

WAITING

She waiteth far beyond my sight,
　　The soul that's meant for me;
　　　　I see her face
　　　　Is gentlest grace,
And sheds around a tender light,
　　But more I cannot see.

She came erewhile to bless my dream,
　　And whispered I must wait;
　　　　But then I woke
　　　　Just as she spoke;
I turned to catch the vision's gleam,
　　But then it was too late.

And now in sleep she comes again
　　To let me mark her face,
　　　　But lingers far,
　　　　Like Fortune's star,
Beyond the circle of my pain
　　She will some time displace.

12

Waiting

Nor eye nor ear nor any sense
 Of mine hath found her out;
  And yet those eyes,
  O, how I prize!
Discovered by a faith intense,
 Will bring the time about.

She dwelleth somewhere in the light
 Of a most homelike heaven,
  Nor any love
  Save that above,
Which she believes for all is right,
 To her was ever given.

She waiteth, yet 'tis I who wait,
 She liveth only free;
  Nor may I seem
  Part of her dream;
And yet some time or soon or late
 She'll come and speak to me.

Some time she'll come to lift my head
 As once she seemed in sleep,
  And bid me rise
  And see those eyes,

Waiting

Not fading when the word is said,
    My treasure e'er to keep.

O, how they seem to guard my days
    Until she surely come!
        Those goddess eyes
        My soul doth prize,
Until I leave these weary ways
    And take her to my home.

I know she waits, that other soul,
    Of all for me the best;
        That sweet unknown
        So precious grown,
Some time will make this being whole—
    Some time will end my quest.

But now I search adown the years
    That only face to see
        Whose living beam
        Will wake my dream:
And I through mist of joyous tears
    Shall know she looks on me!

Cambridge, November 28, 1881.

LOVE'S FLOWER

My love was no sudden-blooming flower
  That burst from the darkness of night,
Rejoicing in a perfect power
  To be and live in the light.

For when it felt in the early days
  The warmth of thy summoning beam,
It hardly dared to turn away
  From its dark and narrow dream.

And when thy smile first fell on my heart
  It could not leap to thy kiss;
I could not claim that light for my part
  Which the wide world must not miss.

So I dared not think it was meant for me,
  And my life was timid and slow;
But love hath now no life but in thee,
  And asketh none other to know.

Cambridge, April, 1882.

THE SONG AND THE DEED

There was never a song that was sung by thee,
But a sweeter one was meant to be.

There was never a deed that was grandly
     done,
But a greater was meant by some earnest one.

For the sweetest voice can never impart
The song that trembles within the heart.

And the brain and hand can never quite do
The thing that the soul has fondly in view.

And hence are the tears and the burdens of
     pain,
For the shining goals are never to gain.

The Song and the Deed

And the real song is ne'er heard by man,
Nor the work ever done for which we plan.

But enough, that a God can hear and see
The song and the deed that were meant to be!

Chicago, February 19, 1895.

LOSS

A little disc of loss
  Doth hang before the eye
And cast its sad eclipse across
  The broad and beauteous sky.

And the creation vast,
  ·Is not as 'twas before —
As if its glory all had passed
  And beauty were no more.

Yet there it beams as broad —
  Its speech is there to learn;
And in the loss, a waiting God
  Giveth new joy to earn!

Cambridge, October 21, 1879.

STARTLING

My love, I loved another maid,
   And yet to you I am true;
I loved her as she passed the street,
   And her dream like image flew;
I loved that other maid, my love,
   Because methought it was *you!*

Cambridge, June 14, 1892.

TO LAKE MICHIGAN

Here have I been full oft before,
  And spent the early evening hour,
And heard the waters' muffled roar,
  And felt the searching of their power.

To thee, fair Lake, I turn again
  To breathe once more thy sweetened breath,
And catch such meaning from thy strain
  As may go with me till my death.

For nears the time when we must part ;
  And thou hast been a friend to me,
And spoken sweetly to my heart,
  And whispered some deep liberty,

What time I left my daily cares
  And felt a portion of thy peace,
Which stole upon me unawares
  And gave me undeserved release.

To Lake Michigan

Oh! may thy soothing spell return
  When I am sundered far away ;
And may such evening rapture yearn
  After the travails of the day —

Come and remind in after years
  How once I used to dream of thee,
And saw the furthering of my tears
  In what my lot was bound to be.

Oh, leastwise, let me not forget
  How, when my days did vainly glide,
I found some promptings in thee yet
  And felt me nobler at thy side.

Chicago, July 31, 1879.

LOST OPPORTUNITY

I stood beside an open gate
  Which showed beyond field after field
Wherein did richest pastures wait,
  Sure-scented though but half-revealed.

I thought me then to enter there,
  Till by some outer calling led ;
I turned my wandering otherwhere
  And found but weariness instead.

And though some gates of promise may
  Ope often on my sight again,
There never greets me by the way,
  Such vista as invited then!

Chicago, June 25, 1879.

THE MESSAGE OF JESUS

Said Jesus, when he came to me,
  "I have no worldly store to give;
I only came that you might see
  The better how to live.

" I point where living waters flow,
  Far wandering from the paths of sin ;
Nor house, nor lands—I only show
  Immortal wealth within."

Said Jesus when his gift I knew :
  "Behold, I am the Way to live;
Tell freely as I told it you :
  I gave that you might give."

Valatic, N. Y.

FUNCTIONS

I said, in a sunny-hearted time,
  "No one there lives but hath somewhat of
    good!"
Beautiful saying to fit into rhyme —
  Beautiful message, but half understood.

Then the years came along with stealthy tread
  And slowly their fingers whitened my hair,
While my motto became as one of the dead,
  Buried amidst my sorrows and care.

And when I recalled it, I thought me so wise
  That I said: "The thought is but fancy of
    youth;
For many a soul is worthless and dies,
  Void of all prophet—I seek but the truth."

Functions

But then I grew weary and longed for repose,
  And sought for the passionless peace of the
    tomb,
Till I seemed all unuseful and lone, and I
    chose
  To sink in the tide of oblivion's gloom.

Then one came to love me, and light burst
    around,
  And I knew all are useful or here or above;
God seeth the sparrow that falls to the ground,
  And every soul merits another soul's love.

Concord, August 2, 1882.

REST

Breathed never fairer evening spell
  Than broods around me at this hour:
Nor ever Nature's parts so well
  Blent into one entrancing power.

And ever doth a gentle breeze
  Slow wander o'er the water's breast,
With message from the outer seas
  That all around is sweetest rest.

Yes, peace is reigning everywhere
  But in the central soul, which sings
And finds for its unrest and care
  No healing in the evening's wings.

But, somehow, seem the waves to say,
  The while they sing the evening psalm,
That some time there will come a day
  When this worn life will be as calm.

Chicago, June 21, 1879.

MY DEBTS

The tender song of passing bird
   Broke in upon my silence lone,
And something in its strain I heard
   Revealed a joy before unknown.
Methought, as soon it flew away,
Its song I never could repay.

Fain had I paid that sudden debt,
   And fed the bird and kept it warm,
And chosen it to be my pet
   And sheltered it from every storm ;
But fell from its enraptured song
No hint of where it might belong.

But from its cadence sweet there fell
   One strain had soothed me into rest.
Had it not whispered just as well,
   My wish could never reach its nest,
To add one comfort to its home
Or give one errand less to roam.

My Debts

So many a life its message sweet
  Drops in upon my weary way —
Some whisper I can ne'er repeat,
  A joy I never can repay.
Like music, of a tender strain,
That soothes, and quick is gone again.

Yes, from the world on every side
  Soft messages are borne to me
Like music caught on mystic tide,
  That swells from Life's mysterious sea.
Though hearing much, I listen well,
I hear what I can never tell.

Great God! how can I e'er repay
  The gift unearned that angels bring,
That through the noise of every day
  Upon me breathe their offering —
The privilege of now and here
To drink the music of the sphere?

My Debts

But more and more they come and sing
   The songs that overswell my debt;
And more and more their burdens bring:
   While giving ne'er, I ever get.
This debt, unpaid, will, by and by,
Imprison me until I die.

Cambridge, January, 1881.

LOVE, THE CROWN OF CREATION

How matchless was Creation's march when
man,
Last summoned, stepped into the foremost
place
And looked the lower orders in the face,
His godlike brow bespeaking him the van!
How vast God's skill, if there had ceased the
plan
With that lone model of the human race!
His Maker's image, set in perfect grace,
With promise of the endless things he can!
But 'twas not meet that man should be alone
In that supremacy, with nought to prove —
No sacrifice, no brotherhood to own,
No tenderness to turn his thoughts above :
Creation lacked its crown until that throne
Was tremulous unto the touch of Love.

1882.

DEATH'S MYSTERY

How far, I wonder, have my dear ones fled
Into the regions hidden from my sight
Helping to people in the realms of light,
With all the countless spirits of the dead,
A mighty world, whereof the prophet said
O'er its fair landscape cometh never night;
Nor sun nor moon shall make its valleys
      bright,
For God himself shall be the Light instead ?
How far, I wonder, have my dear ones gone ?
And yet I must not wonder, but abide
God's purposes till they be fuller grown,
And in the mystery His wisdom guide
My life to waken in the vast Unknown
And find its way to Love's familiar side.

April, 1889.

HARMONY

As in the swelling of some chorus sweet,
Which, many-voiced, pours full upon the ear
Its flood of consonance, we seem to hear
But the fine blending where the voices meet,
Nor reck if in our rapture so replete
We miss the several voice, which fain would
near
Its end of excellence and gain the cheer
That the well-doing of its part may greet:
So in the mystic harmony of life
Makes each one melody, though noisy days
Unfit his hearing; and beyond the strife
The ear of God detects the song we raise,
And waits till through the universe is rife
The glorious climax of our Maker's praise.

Chicago, March 8, 1879.

PITY NOT THE DEAD

O visit not the kingdom of the dead
With one regret for them, for all is gain
That comes in surest meed of joy or pain
And all that takes inevitable stead
Of this short life ; O pity not the dead,
So silent now in death, the quiet brain
Urging no more endeavors that are vain,
And soon to blend it with its earthly bed.
Now doth the soul press forward its career,
With not a step but doth for progress count;
And every wrong and hardship suffered here
Helps on the freedom that doth ever mount
The slope of heavenly growth without a fear,
And every grade hath its refreshing fount.

Chicago, March 27, 1895.

33

ONE MASTER

A Voice came wafted to me from the sea,
Burdened with deep reproof and touched with
      pain,
And as I turned me to the land again
The self-same message echoed unto me:
"What part, O wayward soul, have I in thee?
One purpose only in the world doth reign,
One mighty will, and yet thou dost in vain
Chase forth and yon, as if some fragment, free
To choose thy life apart. Oh, rather find
Thy freedom in My will, and ever shun
The phantom of thy selfishness and bind
Thy conscious life to Mine, no more to run
And do the bidding of the changing mind.
One Master thou canst serve, and only one."

Magnolia, August 13, 1889.

TIRING OF TOYS

Tiring of toys and all his daily glee,
His ruddy face pressing the window pane,
A little boy with health in every vein
Looks out upon the winter wild and free,
And gazes through the whitening storms to
    see
If he who bringeth Christmas gifts again,
Perchance is stealing o'er the dusky plain
To seek the fireside of his nursery.
E'en more the soul whom deeper weariness
Turns from the play of life, to wonder why
It satisfieth not amid the press
Of problems, peers into the baffling sky,
If haply One who more than life can bless
May note his humble window passing by.

Cambridge, December 15, 1880.

IMMANUEL

I came to thee, My child, when night was
    still,
And spoke to thee in thy most secret thought,
With the first knowledge of the struggle
    fraught
Between thy baser and thy purer will;
I came to thee and left thee not until
The path was clear whereof My wisdom
    taught;
And brooding o'er thee, the Eternal Aught,
A sweet submission came thy soul to fill.
And as My spirit leaned upon thee then,
Thou knew'st My name was Duty and My
    way
Looked not unto expedience of men.
Still know, when Duty turns to Love, that day
That I have come and supped with thee
    again,
And but thyself can bid Me stranger stay.

PRINTED BY R. R. DONNELLEY & SONS
COMPANY, AT THE LAKESIDE PRESS,
CHICAGO, UNDER THE DIRECTION
OF STONE & KIMBALL, MDCCCXCV